WALT DISNEY'S

GOOFY

and the MILLER

GROLIER
BOOK CLUB EDITION

There was once an old miller
who had three helpers.
Their names were Goofy, Jim, and Jack.

Goofy was honest and helpful.
He did most of the hard work.
The other two were lazy.
They did not do their fair share.

Goofy carried
heavy sacks of grain
while Jack and Jim
played cards.

And Goofy swept up
while the others loafed.

All alone Goofy pushed and carried
the great barrels of oats
that would be ground into oatmeal.
And he was always the first to come
when the miller called his helpers.

One day the miller said,
"Soon I am going to retire.
I would like to give the mill
to one of you. I want each of you
to go off into the world. The one
who brings me back the finest
horse can have the mill and be
miller when I retire."

The next day Jack and Jim took the path that led to the rich farmlands of the valley.

Goofy took the path
that led to the forest.
"Ha, ha!" laughed the other two.
"He will never find a horse
in the middle of the forest."

Goofy walked and
walked.

He saw birds and
chipmunks.

He stopped to say hello
to a fat frog.

He watched fish jump high out of the water.
And he felt like an acrobat as he walked
on a log to cross the stream.

That night Goofy slept under a tree.
The moon came up, and all the animals
watched over him.

When Goofy awoke the next morning,
an old woman was standing over him.
"What are you doing here?" she asked.
"I am looking for a fine horse
    for the miller," he said.

"Will you help me find wood instead?"
asked the old woman.

"Yes, I will help you,"
said Goofy.

Goofy cheerfully gathered
a large bundle of sticks.

Then he carried the sticks
home for the old woman.

"There is my cottage," she said
as she pointed the way.

Goofy also carried jugs of water
to the cottage for the old woman.
Then he fixed the straw roof so
the rain would not come in.

He chopped wood
for her fireplace.

and he picked apples...

...so she would have
fresh fruit all winter.

"There," said Goofy when he finished,
"now you will be snug all winter long."

"You are very kind," said the old woman.
"Now I will do something for you. Go home,
and in three days I will bring you
the finest horse you have ever seen."

Goofy was surprised, but
he believed the old woman.
He agreed to go straight home.

Goofy waved good-by until the old woman
and her small cottage were out of sight.

As Goofy walked through the forest,
he enjoyed the song of the birds.
He shared his lunch with
the friendly fish, as the frog looked on.

Finally Goofy arrived at the mill.
Jack and Jim had gotten there first.
The miller was admiring
the two beautiful horses they had given him.

Jack had found a horse
that was large and strong.
"A good work horse," said the miller.

Jim's horse was tall and sleek.
"Why, that is a race horse,"
said the miller.
He scratched his beard.
He really did not know
which horse to choose.

"Where is your horse, Goofy?"
asked the miller.

"It will be here in three days," said Goofy.

"Three days?" said Jack and Jim.

"You mean your horse walks so slowly
it will take three days to get here? Ha, ha!"

"Three days is all right with me,"
said the miller. "I will wait.
Now, come on back to the mill.
There is work to be done."

And so once more Goofy was back at work.
He carried the heavy sacks and greased
the mill's wheels so they would not squeak.

He filled the big sacks so fast
that there were clouds of flour around him.
Jim and Jack laughed and laughed.
"Ha, ha! Goofy's horse needs three days
to get here," they said.

But on the morning of the third day
there was the clatter of wheels and
the sound of trumpets.

A fancy blue carriage pulled up
in front of the mill.

A beautiful princess was inside the carriage.

The miller and Jack and Jim
could hardly believe their eyes.

Goofy was already hard at work
and was nowhere to be seen.

The princess leaned out of the window.
The miller tipped his hat to her.
"Where is your helper,"
the princess said to him.
"At your service,"
said Jack and Jim,
bowing low.

But the princess did not want either of them.

Meanwhile the miller was looking
at the horse led by the groom.

Its mane was silky and its coat
was glossy.

The miller admired its strong teeth.

"My," he said. "This is the finest horse
I have ever seen in my life! It must be
the finest horse in the world."

Just then Goofy came
around the corner into the yard,
carrying a sack of flour over
his shoulder.

"There he is! That's the one!"
said the princess, and she
got out of the carriage.

Goofy was surprised.
"Who are you?" he asked.

"I am the old woman
of the forest," she said. "At least,
I WAS. Your kindness broke
a wicked spell. Now I am
a princess again. And this is
the horse I promised to bring you."

"Take him. He is yours," she said.
Goofy took the reins of the horse.
Then he turned to the miller.
"This horse is for you," he said.

"I have never
seen such a
beautiful animal,"
said the miller.
"If this horse
is mine, the mill
is yours, Goofy."

"No, leave the mill
and come with me,"
said the princess.
"You were kind and worked
hard for an ugly old woman.
You asked no reward.
Now you may live happily
all the days of your life."

"Well," said the miller to Jack and Jim, "we can't just stand here. Let's see which one of you is the better worker. To him I will give the mill."

So now the two
had to work
for the first time.

They carried sacks
and pushed barrels...

...and greased
the wheels.

Goofy and the princess
rode off in the carriage
to the castle that stood
where the small cottage had been.
And they lived happily ever after.